MY

MORTAL ENEMY

MY
MORTAL
ENEMY

——

Willa Cather

——

Vintage Books

A DIVISION OF RANDOM HOUSE

NEW YORK

INTRODUCTION

AFTER *My Mortal Enemy* the next novel was to be *Death Comes for the Archbishop,* that most fluent and serene of Willa Cather's elegies. Before it, by a handful of years, there had been the radiance and the supreme ease of *My Ántonia.* In the years between there was a gathering darkness of which *My Mortal Enemy,* in form the most severe and in its implications the most furious of Willa Cather's novels, was the crisis.

Or it is to be seen that the same forces of darkness had been gathering from the beginning and that a series of holding visions culminating in *My Ántonia* had given way. *Alexander's Bridge,* in 1912, a story of a hubristic hero who reached beyond convention for a new freshness and an extra intensity in life and who overreached himself, and then *O Pioneers!* and then *The Song of the Lark,* all quite different in their circumstances and occasions, had all struggled toward an image of poised and indisputable greatness, by which everything that cluttered, everything that was tawdry and cheap and small and restricting, would be subdued. The dark enemy was whatever clutched the individual, and heroism was in dominating it or living through it, enduring at the cost of any personal sacrifice to the point of absolute and untouchable equability. They are austere heroes and heroines of those early novels. The metaphor of striving varies— Alexander is an engineer, Alexandra Bergson of *O Pioneers!* is a pioneer, Thea Kronberg of *The Song of the Lark* is a singer—but the goal is the same. They are in pursuit not of happiness but success. They are in pursuit not of an ideal—ideals contain ideas, and Willa Cather was not an idealogue—but of an integrity, the feel of purity and finality and permanence, beyond all pettiness.

The striving in the early novels is sometimes shrill. "If you love the good thing vitally," Thea Kronberg says, "enough to give up for it all that one must give up, then you must hate the cheap thing just as hard! I tell you there is such a thing as creative hate!" The shrillness measures the severity of the striving, and compromises it. But then, after striving, there was no such desperation or struggle at all to Ántonia Shimerda, whose success is simply the endurance of her vitality. Because she is, because she exists, the enemy is routed. The novel is her magnificent stillness—there is in her commonest gesture, the narrator says, something immemorial and universal and true, and that really is the case—and the enemy is reduced by her to scampering trivialities. There is a melancholy always just behind her, a suggestion of cultural riches lost in her transplanting from Bohemia to this new country, of trials imposed by a capricious fate. But nothing really can hurt her. Not her toil, not the townsmen who exploit her, least of all the mechanical little man who seduces her. Not love, either, nor hate. Her domain for creation is the Nebraska soil that she makes into a farm, and she is its equivalent in her lastingness and her gift of life and her incorruptibility. And Ántonia is absorbed, indeed, in the huge, solid, still image to which all the novel comes, to which Willa Cather after many trials had come, of a plow silhouetted against the setting Nebraska sun.

It was an image of unimpeachable grandeur. But then it was as well apparently anachronistic. The day of greatness on the Nebraska frontier, that last of the agricultural frontiers, had lasted only a moment of the mid-1880's, and had been suddenly eclipsed by drought and depression and finance capitalism. Or perhaps it had never been at all. Nothing in Willa Cather's own early life on the Nebraska frontier suggests the possibility of Ántonia's elemental piety. Everything, to the contrary, suggests that she found her few years in Red Cloud, Nebraska, population in the 1880's about 1,000, unbearably constricting. Allowing even a great deal for normal youthful rebelliousness—she was eleven years old when she was taken from a farm in Virginia to Nebraska, and seventeen when she left Red Cloud for the University at Lincoln—she was markedly defiant, markedly bent on escape. Her companions in the village were the old men and women, anyone whose real life had been elsewhere. Her allegiances were to the Europeans scattered among the population, whose lives hinted a substantial and ancient and non-proscriptive culture. The village in all her Nebraska novels was to be the source of all corruptions, its dominant Anglo-Saxon inhabitants narrow, ignorant, imposing, convention-ridden, and exploitative, and she had herself opposed it in what ways one supposes she could. She wore her hair assertively short and wore clothes assertively mannish. She held unconventional ideas about religion, and she lectured her Baptist neighbors on the necessity of scientific investigation over their superstition. And most significantly, in that squeezing village she bent herself to a notion of greatness.

The village commanded defiance and Ántonia's easy supremacy had not been available to her. The village was not strictly the frontier, but one may doubt that there was really much distance between, only just enough, perhaps, for Willa Cather to make a heroic myth of the frontier. But in any event by 1918, when she published *My Ántonia*, the great frontier had really and clearly long ago been captured by the village. The pioneers had not endured. Their great achievements had been inherited by the lesser men who were their sons, whose natural home was the village. Everything subversive of greatness had won out. The degeneration of the frontier was to be the explicit theme now of her next few novels, treated in each successively with more reserve, the terms of the defeat seen in each novel successively to be of greater dimension.

In *One of Ours* in 1922 the hero does escape the Nebraska farm and village, both now populated by prohibitionists and farm implements salesmen and prim evangelists, but only by the miraculous and ironic intervention of the World War. More than that, though he dies for it on the Western Front, he becomes a hero of sensibility. *His* war is for the greatness that is in European culture and that was once in the frontier, and so he has opportunity to be a last pioneer. But he is the last. The next novel, *A Lost Lady*, is the unmitigated process of degeneration itself. The lady is a great lady while she is married to one of the great pioneers, in this case one of the men who had built the railroad. She is lost when he dies, and what she loses is not merely sensibility, which in fact she preserves, but the nerve and the moral rectitude and the courage without which her ladylike sensibility is merely prettiness. She becomes the property of the next generation in the person of a manipulating lawyer who had once not dared to walk in her garden. And the next novel, *The Professor's House,* brings this corroding malignity of modernism into the most normal domestic affections. The professor has a wife, a good wife, and a daughter whom he loves, but they are of the present, adepts of easy comforts. Their skill is in spending money. His own proper life is in the heroic frontier past. It is that which sustains him, and when his great scholarly study of it is finished, he is finished. The love of his family notwithstanding, their life in this time is not his life, and he is ready for death.

In her prefatory note to a book of essays in 1936, a book she belligerently called *Not Under Forty* because it was not to be read by anyone under forty, Willa Cather was to say that "The world broke in two in 1922 or thereabouts," and she made it clear that she had made her own house in the world before. The year of *One of Ours* was 1922. It was also, it happened, the year that T. S. Eliot published *The Waste Land,* and it was the year of E. E. Cummings' *The Enormous Room* and of Sinclair Lewis' *Babbitt,* and it was just a couple of years after Edith Wharton's *The Age of Innocence* and H. L. Mencken's *The American Credo,* and a couple of years before Ellen Glasgow's *Barren Ground*—all of them assaults on modernism, in various tempers and modes, more or less explicit, by persons of a series of generations. Nothing would have pleased Willa Cather less, certainly, than to have found herself part of a literary movement. Or she would have found the fact irrelevant. Her way was absolutely independent devotion to her art. Her great masters were Shakespeare and Flaubert, and she had taken practical lessons from Henry James and Sarah Orne Jewett, never from any of the excited literary factionalists. But in fact what she observed was being observed by most serious writers. In 1922 or thereabouts some personal possibility of grace, of coherence, of achievement, or personal heroism had been defeated in America—that was, for instance, what Ezra Pound, the most clamorous factionalist of them all, had meant when in 1920 he said of his Mauberly that his true Penelope was Flaubert. There was a rigor and an austerity and a dedication missing from this modern America. The defeat surely had something to do with the sudden new wealth of a country suddenly beyond its youth. It had something to do with the happy post-war disillusion that was the philosophical basis for iconoclasm, hedonism, and that literary fiction, the Younger Generation. But whatever it had to do with, not only the conservatives of an older generation, but the young radical iconoclasts themselves agreed on the wasteland as the image of modern times. What Willa Cather's Professor St. Peter discovered in the present is very much Babbittry, or the same thing made more intimate and therefore more crushing. Or her Professor who discovered that the present is the time of death, was not very different from the protagonist of *The Waste Land* whose true life was in a medieval legend.

And the three novels of the 1920's in which Willa Cather tracked the decline of the Nebraska frontier made still another instance, recorded in another parish, of modern degeneration. That last agricultural frontier had also become a wasteland. That was the objective fact, and the fact had social and political and cultural implications. But still the mode of her apprehension of it is everything, and her response to it was unique. It had no public implications for her. The tone of the new generation was by and large irony, or outright shock that such Babbittry or such a wasteland could be, and despite the negatives in which it spoke, its purpose was forward-looking and progressive. It meant to stir things up, to effect reforms, to set society and politics and culture right. Or the tone of such a writer as Ellen Glasgow, Willa Cather's exact contemporary, was by and large romantic irony. Ellen Glasgow's aristocrats had declined into the time of modernism and she exposed their decline but loved them nevertheless. Or the searching vision of an elder, Edith Wharton, had come to rest, in *The Age of Innocence,* in retrospective affection, just bolstered by a modern sharpness. The new generation was censorious, with a purpose. The older generation watched the passing of the old with nostalgia, just made a bit acid by a sense of the new.

The tone of Willa Cather's apprehension was neither ironic nor nostalgic. And in fact her purpose was just the opposite of, say, that of T. S. Eliot. Eliot made a wasteland populated by bored, sterile, desiccated, valueless automatons and submitted it, by a process of interweaving myths, to the criticism of the heroic past. Willa Cather had from the beginning made heroic myths—myths rescued from the crushing clutter of the present, or myths of the heroic past which, it happened, could not prevent what she was to call "the noisy push of the present." It was the past she looked at, and not the present at all except where some value of the past miraculously could spring out of it, or where it intruded. The past was, simply, where she located greatness, and greatness was her constant subject, and not degeneration. It was not even actual, or her personal history that she recorded —she was not, after all, a "historical novelist"—but a country that her imagination could conceive to contain images of greatness. The three Nebraska novels of the 1920's track degeneration, and their effect is not of the rush of the new mediocrity, not of degeneration, but of the quantity of the loss. *The Waste Land* discovered the present and was hortatory. Willa Cather created a past and was elegiac.

Those three Nebraska novels record, in a way, her loss of a subject. The frontier had in fact yielded to

the obtrusive present, and it must have been as difficult
for Willa Cather to locate again its greatness as it
would have been inconceivable for Sinclair Lewis to
imagine the pioneering days of Gopher Prairie. And
so she was put to the critical labor of finding a purer
past, one that would stay past and not decay into the
present, one that could propose images that would last
forever. Like Eliot, ironically enough, and at about
the same time, she discovered an aesthetic proposed
by Catholicism. She was not a Catholic. It was not
the doctrinal Church that attracted her. But there
was a magnitude in Catholicism that was sufficient to
her, and a tradition in it that had preserved itself
whole through much change, and a tradition so ancient as to be effectively out of time.

Death Comes for the Archbishop, the first of her
two novels of Catholic inspiration, is a novel without
plot, and the plot of the other, *Shadows on the Rock,*
is the merest sketch. Plots occur in time, depend on
change, and it was precisely an image of changeless-
ness that she wanted. And not that image that Eliot
came to name "the still point of the turning world,"
but something that would clearly dominate the turning world—the aesthetic that Henry Adams had de-
veloped out of Catholicism was much closer to her
own—something with landscape to it. And the vast
landscape of *Death Comes for the Archbishop,* the
deserts and mountains and mesas of the Southwest, is
scarcely so much the setting of the novel as it is the

condition of the two emissaries of the Church who are set to move through it. As there is in the priests, there is change, even fluidity within, a varying distribution of accents and light. But its aspect as a whole, as it is that of the priests, is of a largeness and solidity and serene fixity. The novel, indeed, isn't a novel at all, but a legend or a vision of a great, severe quietude, quite removed from and superior to all mortality.

For it was not after all the peculiar historical circumstances of the present that constituted the enemy. Willa Cather's mode was elegy, and as it must be for all elegists, the enemy was time, mortality, itself. The enemy therefore was everything that is a part of mortality, including that modernism that had sapped the frontier and including as well all domestic, mortal feelings. Professor St. Peter had discovered himself wishing for death when the emphasis of his life shifted from the past to the prospect not only of mean present-day commercialism, but to the prospect also of his being merely a husband and a father. There is destruction in such mortal love. It is antagonistic to grandeur. There is in *Death Comes for the Archbishop* a libertine priest, a remarkably good man, who argues the needs of the flesh, and the Archbishop, rather than punish what he perceives to be unworthiness and uncleanliness, can wait for the priest to die. It is the success of the Church that it survives mere mortal goodness, as it is the success of the land that it is unmarked by human habitants. Love, charity, goodness, kindness—they are as much in time as modernism and therefore equally corrupting, only perhaps more insidious because not so apparently evil.

In an essay of 1936 on the fiction of Katherine Mansfield, Willa Cather was to remark that "human relationships are the tragic necessity of human life; that they can never be wholly satisfactory, that every ego is half the time greedily seeking them, and half the time pulling away from them." And it is the struggle to get beyond the necessity of human relationships that is the secret history of all Willa Cather's novels, only as time went on, as the struggle turned, one supposes, more desperate, its nature became more apparent. After *My Ántonia* there is a gathering darkness of which *My Mortal Enemy* is the crisis, and in each of the novels between those two the enemy is, successively, a more intimate part of the hero. In *One of Ours* the particular enemy is still for the most part the aggressively ignorant village, and *One of Ours* is still for the most part one of those 1920's novels of the "village virus." In *A Lost Lady* the enemy is the village, but it is also the modern life that the heroine after all must live. In *The Professor's House* it is the family, and the Professor is put to the altogether impossible choice between his artifice of the past and the wife whom he does love. In *My Mortal Enemy*, then, it is friendship and love, human relationship itself.

Willa Cather wrote *My Mortal Enemy* in the early months of 1925, in the interval while *The Professor's*

House was being put through publication, and it is clear that she was making another, now sterner attempt at the same thematic material. Professor St. Peter had had his artifice of another life and he had also had money, by which he could make at least an uneasy compromise with his family. Moreover, at the last moment he had been saved from death and from thoughts of death by an old woman out of the frontier past who was seasoned to endurance. He had not had to live through his marriage, and he is saved in his critical perception of it now from the ultimate despair. What if a person even, or especially, of St. Peter's intensity of character were to be submitted to other circumstances and conditions, to a marriage contracted in passionate youth that could not afterwards be evaded? What if there were no device by which another life might be accomplished, and what if there were no money? The story of Myra Henshawe is, briefly, that of a woman who chooses love over all other possibilities, and who suffers for it. She suffers not heart-break—poetry should not attempt to do any heart-breaking, Willa Cather was to remark—but diminution. She purchases at the end, by a harsh sacrifice of all human affections, a desperate moment of greatness.

The novel, a recent critic says, is "the least likable" of Willa Cather's works—and it probably is, in the way that *Coriolanus* is perhaps the least "likable" of Shakespeare's plays—and Myra Henshawe, the same critic says, is "thoroughly unpleasant." She is, and that is a mark of the novel's strictness. Her charm is, or was, in the youthful abandon with which she gave up a fortune for romance. It is what a heroine should do. She and her runaway marriage, the narrator tells us at the very beginning, have for years been the only interesting topics of gossip at family dinners, and it is clear that her Aunt Lydia has devoted her life to the memory of the night Myra eloped. But the charm of that moment cannot be, and is not, permanent. It is preserved in Aunt Lydia's gossip, but for Myra the pleasant gesture meant a marriage and, in the most practical terms, a commitment to love. Her subsequent life has been as happy as that of most people, Aunt Lydia says, though apparently she thinks such reflection somehow beside the point, and only the narrator sees the slight tarnishing irony in it, sees that Myra's gesture, which had been larger than most people's, should have earned her a happiness more brilliant than other people's.

Her commitment to love, we come to see, has yielded her a life somewhat less happy than that of other people, though happiness is indeed not quite relevant to her. The novel isn't an inverted fairy tale, of the princess who must, princess or no, accommodate herself to a daily life and growing old. Myra isn't a romantic heroine, but imperious and equipped with a taste for greatness. And what we see in the first part of the novel is Myra, with what the narrator calls her something "compelling, passionate, overmastering," extravagantly, against frustrating circumstances and with a secret notion of her folly, repeating her commitment. Myra in middle age has become a friend to young lovers. She is nearly always, her husband complains, helping a love affair along. She is at pains to put the best romantic appearance on her own marriage. She dresses brilliantly, as befits a great lover. And she devotes herself absolutely, because it is part of loving, to her friendships. She is one of the great few who know what friendship means. But underneath all her actions there is a sense that the activity itself is insufficient, that it can't secure for her what her nature demands. She has behind her a record, not to be blinked, of friendships betrayed. It is suggested that she knows, moreover, that her husband is unfaithful to her. And as for the lovers she is helping along, she thinks that "very likely hell will come of it."

There is about Myra, and that is also a part of the novel's strictness, something not merely unpleasant but disproportionate; the intensity of her character is superior to her materials, and so her grand loving has become compulsive. Nevertheless she is sustained while she has a certain amount of youthfulness and a certain amount of money. In the second part of the novel these are taken from her, and she is left with her commitment pure, and the lesson of her failure. The friends are gone. In their place are the upstairs neighbors whose every movement beats on her consciousness. "Why," says Myra, who has been a great friend and therefore intimate with human existence, "Why should I have the details of their stupid, messy existence thrust upon me all day long, and half the night?" She regrets bitterly now her sacrifice of a fortune. Money has might and it does endure. The money that was to have been hers has actually gone to found a convent, and it is implicit that it is a convent that Myra wants, a place of quiet but absolute strength and dignity. And most of all she regrets her marriage, now.

In her old age, she says at one point, she has lost the power to love. In fact, however, she has not suffered loss but, rather, defeat by love. Her husband, who is devoted to her, is now unbearable to her, because he is the source of her defeat. She and her husband, she tells the narrator, have been great lovers and as well great enemies. They have done each other harm. Their marriage has been their ruin. They have destroyed each other. And what in their marriage was destructive, though she does not explicitly draw the conclusion herself, is what is destructive in "messy existence" itself. Myra turns, in this savage, bitter age of hers, to what is not messy. She is drawn to a particular bare headland on the Pacific slope where there is silence and vista and where she can imagine the first cold, bright streak of dawn over the water—it is in that setting, rather than in her husband's home, that she chooses to die. And she turns to the Catholicism of her youth. Catholicism is not a dogma for her, but, as it was to be in *Death Comes for the Archbishop*, it is an aesthetic. Religion is that in which seeking is finding, desire is fulfillment, and so it has none of the tragic restlessness of human relations.

The Pacific headland and Catholicism have an incontestable greatness and endurance which human relationship, even at the highest pitch of love, can't have. When Myra dies she faces her husband with a "terrible judgment": "Why must I die like this, alone with my mortal enemy?" There is a deep pun in the phrase. Her husband is her enemy because he is the source for her of human relationship, of that which passes without fulfillment, of mortality.

For Willa Cather herself, of course, the source of personal greatness and immortality was her craft, and she went at it with an enormous energy and intelligence. There were others at the time of her greatest production who also made a religion of craftsmanship —Gertrude Stein, who was her exact contemporary, Ezra Pound, Hemingway—but next to Willa Cather they seem sloganeers. She quite alone, and without making a public campaign of it, put in the work and achieved a relentless purity of style. Never so pure and never so relentless as in *My Mortal Enemy*. It is a book made with the utmost rigor, and it is therefore the perfect expression of Myra Henshawe. Like Myra, the novel makes a raid on all amplitudes, all mere pleasantness, and all sloppinesses. The novel is not without its structural curiosities. The narrator wanders in and out of perspective and acts sometimes as a naïve observer and sometimes as the author's spokesman. An eighteen-year-old lady journalist who looks very much like Willa Cather herself at eighteen wanders twice into the story without apparent function. It is not so surely composed a novel as *A Lost Lady*. But in no other novel did Willa Cather ever so strenuously grasp and compress her matter. As no other novel required of her such strenuosity.

The story of Myra Henshawe must have been a personal crisis. There is no knowing for sure because there is available no record other than the novel. It doesn't much matter. It is that crisis in which all merely mortal life must be measured by the terms of real greatness.

MARCUS KLEIN

Barnard College 1961

PART

I

I

I FIRST met Myra Henshawe when I was fifteen, but I had known about her ever since I could remember anything at all. She and her runaway marriage were the theme of the most interesting, indeed the only interesting, stories that were told in our family, on holidays or at family dinners. My mother and aunts still heard from Myra Driscoll, as they called her, and Aunt Lydia occasionally went to New York to visit her. She had been the brilliant and attractive figure among the friends of their girlhood, and her life had been as exciting and varied as ours was monotonous.

Though she had grown up in our town, Parthia, in southern Illinois, Myra Henshawe never, after her elopement, came back but once. It was in the year when I was finishing High School, and she must then have been a woman of forty-five. She came in the early autumn, with brief notice by telegraph. Her husband, who had a position in the New York offices of an Eastern railroad, was coming West on business, and they were going to stop over for two days in Parthia. He was to stay at the Parthian, as our new hotel was called, and Mrs. Henshawe would stay with Aunt Lydia.

I was a favourite with my Aunt Lydia. She had three big sons, but no daughter, and she thought my mother scarcely appreciated me. She was always, therefore, giving me what she called "advantages," on the side. My mother and sister were asked to dinner at Aunt Lydia's on the night of the Henshawes' arrival, but she had whispered to me: "I want you to come in early, an hour or so before the others, and get acquainted with Myra."

That evening I slipped quietly in at my aunt's front door, and while I was taking off my wraps in the hall I could see, at the far end of the parlour, a short, plump woman in a black velvet dress, seated upon the sofa and softly playing on Cousin Bert's guitar. She must have heard me, and, glancing up, she saw my reflection in a mirror; she put down the guitar, rose, and stood to await my approach. She stood markedly and pointedly still, with her shoulders back and her head lifted, as if to remind me that it was my business to get to her as quickly as possible and present myself as best I could. I was not accustomed to formality of any sort, but by her attitude she succeeded in conveying this idea to me.

I hastened across the room with so much bewilderment and concern in my face that she gave a short, commiserating laugh as she held out to me her plump, charming little hand.

"Certainly this must be Lydia's dear Nellie, of whom I have heard so much! And you must be fifteen now, by my mournful arithmetic—am I right?"

What a beautiful voice, bright and gay and carelessly kind—but she continued to hold her head up haughtily. She always did this on meeting people—partly, I think, because she was beginning to have a double chin and was sensitive about it. Her deep-set, flashing grey eyes seemed to be taking me in altogether—estimating me. For all that she was no taller than I, I felt quite overpowered by her—and stupid, hopelessly clumsy and stupid. Her black hair was done high on her head, *à la* Pompadour, and there were curious, zigzag, curly streaks of glistening white in it, which made it look like the fleece of a Persian goat or some animal that bore silky fur. I could not meet the playful curiosity of her eyes at all, so I fastened my gaze upon a necklace of carved amethysts she wore inside the square-cut neck of her dress. I suppose I stared, for she said suddenly: "Does this necklace annoy you? I'll take it off if it does."

I was utterly speechless. I could feel my cheeks burning. Seeing that she had hurt me, she was sorry, threw her arm impulsively about me, drew me into the corner of the sofa and sat down beside me.

"Oh, we'll get used to each other! You see, I prod you because I'm certain that Lydia and your mother have spoiled you a little. You've been overpraised to me. It's all very well to be clever, my dear, but you mustn't be solemn about it—nothing is more tiresome. Now, let us get acquainted. Tell me about the things you like best; that's the short cut to friendship. What do you like best in Parthia? The old Driscoll place? I knew it!"

By the time her husband came in I had begun to think she was going to like me. I wanted her to, but I felt I didn't have half a chance with her; her charming, fluent voice, her clear light enunciation bewildered me. And I was never sure whether she was making fun of me or of the thing we were talking about. Her sarcasm was so quick, so fine at the point—it was like being touched by a metal so cold that one doesn't know whether one is burned or chilled. I was fascinated, but very ill at ease, and I was glad when Oswald Henshawe arrived from the hotel.

He came into the room without taking off his

overcoat and went directly up to his wife, who rose and kissed him. Again I was some time in catching up with the situation; I wondered for a moment whether they might have come down from Chicago on different trains; for she was clearly glad to see him—glad not merely that he was safe and had got round on time, but because his presence gave her lively personal pleasure. I was not accustomed to that kind of feeling in people long married.

Mr. Henshawe was less perplexing than his wife, and he looked more as I had expected him to look. The prominent bones of his face gave him a rather military air; a broad, rugged forehead, high cheek-bones, a high nose, slightly arched. His eyes, however, were dark and soft, curious in shape—exactly like half-moons—and he wore a limp, drooping moustache, like an Englishman. There was something about him that suggested personal bravery, magnanimity, and a fine, generous way of doing things.

"I am late," he explained, "because I had some difficulty in dressing. I couldn't find my things."

His wife looked concerned for a moment, and

then began to laugh softly. "Poor Oswald! You were looking for your new dress shirts that bulge in front. Well, you needn't! I gave them to the janitor's son."

"The janitor's son?"

"Yes. To Willy Bunch, at home. He's probably wearing one to an Iroquois ball to-night, and that's the right place for it."

Mr. Henshawe passed his hand quickly over his smooth, iron-grey hair. "You gave away my six new shirts?"

"Be sure I did. You shan't wear shirts that give you a bosom, not if we go to the poorhouse. You know I can't bear you in ill-fitting things."

Oswald looked at her with amusement, incredulity, and bitterness. He turned away from us with a shrug and pulled up a chair. "Well, all I can say is, what a windfall for Willy!"

"That's the way to look at it," said his wife teasingly. "And now try to talk about something that might conceivably interest Lydia's niece. I promised Liddy to make a salad dressing."

I was left alone with Mr. Henshawe. He had a pleasant way of giving his whole attention to a young person. He "drew one out" better than his wife had done, because he did not frighten one so much. I liked to watch his face, with its outstanding bones and languid, friendly eyes—that perplexing combination of something hard and something soft. Soon my mother and uncle and my boy cousins arrived. When the party was complete I could watch and enjoy the visitors without having to think of what I was going to say next. The dinner was much gayer than family parties usually are. Mrs. Henshawe seemed to remember all the old stories and the old jokes that had been asleep for twenty years.

"How good it is," my mother exclaimed, "to hear Myra laugh again!"

Yes, it was good. It was sometimes terrible, too, as I was to find out later. She had an angry laugh, for instance, that I still shiver to remember. Any stupidity made Myra laugh—I was destined to hear that one very often! Untoward circumstances, accidents, even disasters, provoked her mirth. And it was always mirth, not hysteria; there was a spark of zest and wild humour in it.

2

THE BIG stone house, in its ten-acre park of trees and surrounded by a high, wrought-iron fence, in which Myra Driscoll grew up, was still, in my time, the finest property in Parthia. At John Driscoll's death it went to the Sisters of the Sacred Heart, and I could remember it only as a convent. Myra was an orphan, and had been taken into this house as a very little girl and brought up by her great-uncle.

John Driscoll made his fortune employing contract labour in the Missouri swamps. He retired from business early, returned to the town where he had been a poor boy, and built a fine house in which he took great pride. He lived in what was considered great splendour in those days. He kept fast horses, and bred a trotter that made a national record. He bought silver instruments for the town band, and paid the salary of the band-master. When the band went up to serenade him on his birthday and on holidays, he called the boys in and treated them to his best whisky. If Myra gave a ball or a garden-party, the band furnished the music. It was, indeed, John Driscoll's band.

Myra, as my aunt often said, had everything: dresses and jewels, a fine riding horse, a Stein-way piano. Her uncle took her back to Ireland with him, one summer, and had her painted by a famous painter. When they were at home, in Parthia, his house was always open to the young people of the town. Myra's good looks and high spirits gratified the old man's pride. Her wit was of the kind that he could understand, native and racy, and none too squeamish. She was very fond of him, and he knew it. He was a coarse old codger, so unlettered that he made a poor showing with a pen. It was always told of him that when he became president of our national bank, he burned a lot of the treasury notes sent up to his house for him to sign, because he had "spoiled the sig-nay-ture." But he knew a great deal about men and their motives. In his own way he was picturesque, and Myra appreciated it—not many girls would have done so. Indeed, she was a good deal like him; the blood tie was very strong. There was never a serious disagreement between them until it came to young Henshawe.

Oswald Henshawe was the son of a German girl of good family, and an Ulster Protestant whom Driscoll detested; there was an old grudge of some kind between the two men. This Ulsterman was poor and impractical, a wandering schoolmaster, who had charge for a while of the High School in Parthia, and afterwards taught in smaller towns about. Oswald put himself through Harvard with very little help from his parents. He was not taken account of in our town until he came home from college, a handsome and promising young man. He and Myra met as if for the first time, and fell in love with each other. When old Driscoll found that Oswald was calling on his niece, he forbade him the house. They continued to meet at my grandfather's, however, under the protection of my Aunt Lydia. Driscoll so persecuted the boy that he felt there was no chance for him in Parthia. He roused himself and went to New York. He stayed there two years without coming home, sending his letters to Myra through my aunt.

All Myra's friends were drawn into the web of her romance; half a dozen young men understudied for Oswald so assiduously that her uncle might have thought she was going to marry any one of them. Oswald, meanwhile, was pegging away in New York, at a time when salaries were small and advancement was slow. But he managed to get on, and in two years he was in a position to marry. He wrote to John Driscoll, telling him his resources and prospects, and asked him for his niece's hand. It was then that Driscoll had it out with Myra. He did not come at her in a tantrum, as he had done before, but confronted her with a cold, business proposition. If she mar-

ried young Henshawe, he would cut her off without a penny. He could do so, because he had
never adopted her. If she did not, she would in-
herit two-thirds of his property—the remaining
third was to go to the church. "And I advise ye
to think well," he told her. "It's better to be a
stray dog in this world than a man without money.
I've tried both ways, and I know. A poor
man stinks, and God hates him."

Some months after this conversation, Myra
went out with a sleighing party. They drove her
to a neighbouring town where Oswald's father
had a school, and where Oswald himself had quietly arrived the day before. There, in the presence of his parents and of Myra's friends, they
were married by the civil authority, and they
went away on the Chicago express, which came
through at two in the morning.

When I was a little girl my Aunt Lydia used
to take me for a walk along the broad stone flag-
ging that ran all the way around the old Driscoll
grounds. Through the high iron fence we could
see the Sisters, out for recreation, pacing two and
two under the apple-trees. My aunt would tell
me again about that thrilling night (probably the

most exciting in her life), when Myra Driscoll
came down that path from the house, and out of
those big iron gates, for the last time. She had
wanted to leave without taking anything but the
clothes she wore—and indeed she walked out of
the house with nothing but her muff and her
porte-monnaie in her hands. My prudent aunt,
however, had put her toilet articles and some linen
into a travelling-bag, and thrown it out of the back
window to one of the boys stationed under an
apple-tree.

"I'll never forget the sight of her, coming down
that walk and leaving a great fortune behind
her," said Aunt Lydia. "I had gone out to join
the others before she came—she preferred to
leave the house alone. We girls were all in the
sleighs and the boys stood in the snow holding
the horses. We had begun to think she had weak-
ened, or maybe gone to the old man to try to move
him. But we saw by the lights behind when the
front door opened and shut, and here she came,
with her head high, and that quick little bounc-
ing step of hers. Your Uncle Rob lifted her into
the sleigh, and off we went. And that hard old
man was as good as his word. Her name wasn't

mentioned in his will. He left it all to the Catholic Church and to institutions."

"But they've been happy, anyhow?" I sometimes asked her.

"Happy? Oh, yes! As happy as most people."

That answer was disheartening; the very point of their story was that they should be much happier than other people.

When I was older I used to walk around the Driscoll place alone very often, especially on spring days, after school, and watch the nuns pacing so mildly and measuredly among the blossoming trees where Myra used to give garden-parties and have the band to play for her. I thought of the place as being under a spell, like the Sleeping Beauty's palace; it had been in a trance, or lain in its flowers like a beautiful corpse, ever since that winter night when Love went out of the gates and gave the dare to Fate. Since then, chanting and devotions and discipline, and the tinkle of little bells that seemed forever calling the Sisters in to prayers.

I knew that this was not literally true; old John Driscoll had lived on there for many years after the flight of his niece. I myself could remember his funeral—remember it very vividly—though I was not more than six years old when it happened. I sat with my parents in the front of the gallery, at the back of the church that the old man had enlarged and enriched during the latter days of his life. The high altar blazed with hundreds of candles, the choir was entirely filled by the masses of flowers. The bishop was there, and a flock of priests in gorgeous vestments. When the pall-bearers arrived, Driscoll did not come to the church; the church went to him. The bishop and clergy went down the nave and met that great black coffin at the door, preceded by the cross and boys swinging cloudy censers, followed by the choir chanting to the organ. They surrounded, they received, they seemed to assimilate into the body of the church, the body of old John Driscoll. They bore it up to the high altar on a river of colour and incense and organ-tone; they claimed it and enclosed it.

In after years, when I went to other funerals, stark and grim enough, I thought of John Driscoll as having escaped the end of all flesh; it was as if he had been translated, with no dark conclusion to the pageant, no "night of the grave"

about which our Protestant preachers talked.
From the freshness of roses and lilies, from the
glory of the high altar, he had gone straight to
the greater glory, through smoking censers and
candles and stars.

After I went home from that first glimpse of
the real Myra Henshawe, twenty-five years older
than I had always imagined her, I could not help
feeling a little disappointed. John Driscoll and his
niece had suddenly changed places in my mind,
and he had got, after all, the more romantic part.
Was it not better to get out of the world with such
pomp and dramatic splendour than to linger on in
it, having to take account of shirts and railway
trains, and getting a double chin into the bargain?
The Henshawes were in Parthia three days,
and when they left, it was settled that I was to go
on to New York with Aunt Lydia for the Christmas holidays. We were to stay at the old Fifth
Avenue Hotel, which, as Myra said, was only a
stone's throw from their apartment, "if at any
time a body was to feel disposed to throw one.
Liddy!"

3

MY AUNT LYDIA and I arrived at the Jersey City station on the day before Christmas —a soft, grey December morning, with a little snow falling. Myra Henshawe was there to meet us; very handsome, I thought, as she came walking rapidly up the platform, her plump figure swathed in furs—a fur hat on her head, with a single narrow garnet feather sticking out behind, like the pages' caps in old story-books. She was not alone. She was attended by a tall, elegant young man in a blue-grey ulster. He had one arm through hers, and in the other hand he carried a walking-stick.

"This is Ewan Gray," said Mrs. Henshawe, after she had embraced us. "Doubtless you have seen him play in Chicago. He is meeting an early train, too, so we planned to salute the morn together, and left Oswald to breakfast alone."

The young man took our hand-luggage and walked beside me to the ferryboat, asking polite questions about our trip. He was a Scotchman, of an old theatrical family, a handsome fellow, with a broad, fair-skinned face, sand-coloured hair and moustache, and fine grey eyes, deep-set and melancholy, with black lashes. He took us up to the deck of the ferry, and then Mrs. Henshawe told him he had better leave us. "You must be there when Esther's train gets in—and remember, you are to bring her to dine with us to-morrow night. There will be no one else."

"Thank you, Myra." He stood looking down at her with a grateful, almost humble expression, holding his soft hat against his breast, while the snow-flakes fell about his head. "And may I call in for a few moments to-night, to show you something?"

She laughed as if his request pleased her. "Something for her, I expect? Can't you trust your own judgment?"

"You know I never do," he said, as if that were an old story.

She gave him a little push. "Do put your hat on, or you'll greet Esther with a sneeze. Run along."

She watched him anxiously as he walked away, and groaned: "Oh, the deliberation of him! If I could only make him hurry once. You'll hear all about him later, Nellie. You'll have to see a good deal of him, but you won't find it a hardship, I trust!"

The boat was pulling out, and I was straining my eyes to catch, through the fine, reluctant snow, my first glimpse of the city we were approaching. We passed the *Wilhelm der Grosse* coming up the river under tug, her sides covered with ice after a stormy crossing, a flock of sea gulls in her wake. The snow blurred everything a little, and the buildings on the Battery all ran together—

looked like an enormous fortress with a thousand windows. From the mass, the dull gold dome of the *World* building emerged like a ruddy autumn moon at twilight.

From the Twenty-third Street station we took the crosstown car—people were economical in those days—to the Fifth Avenue Hotel. After we had unpacked and settled our things, we went across the Square to lunch at Purcell's, and there Mrs. Henshawe told us about Ewan Gray. He was in love with one of her dearest friends, Esther Sinclair, whose company was coming into New York for the holidays. Though he was so young, he had, she said, "a rather spotty past," and Miss Sinclair, who was the daughter of an old New England family and had been properly brought up, couldn't make up her mind whether he was stable enough to marry. "I don't dare advise her, though I'm so fond of him. You can see; he's just the sort of boy that women pick up and run off into the jungle with. But he's never wanted to marry before; it might be the making of him. He's distractedly in love—goes about like a sleep-walker. Still, I couldn't bear it if anything cruel happened to Esther."

Aunt Lydia and Myra were going to do some shopping. When we went out into Madison Square again, Mrs. Henshawe must have seen my wistful gaze, for she stopped short and said: "How would Nellie like it if we left her here, and picked her up as we come back? That's our house, over there, second floor—so you won't be far from home. To me this is the real heart of the city; that's why I love living here." She waved to me and hurried my aunt away.

Madison Square was then at the parting of the ways; had a double personality, half commercial, half social, with shops to the south and residences on the north. It seemed to me so neat, after the raggedness of our Western cities; so protected by good manners and courtesy—like an open-air drawing-room. I could well imagine a winter dancing party being given there, or a reception for some distinguished European visitor.

The snow fell lightly all the afternoon, and friendly old men with brooms kept sweeping the paths—very ready to talk to a girl from the coun-

try, and to brush off a bench so that she could sit
down. The trees and shrubbery seemed well-
groomed and sociable, like pleasant people. The
snow lay in clinging folds on the bushes, and out-
lined every twig of every tree—a line of white
upon a line of black. Madison Square Garden,
new and spacious then, looked to me so light and
fanciful, and Saint Gaudens' Diana, of which
Mrs. Henshawe had told me, stepped out freely
and fearlessly into the grey air. I lingered long
by the intermittent fountain. Its rhythmical
splash was like the voice of the place. It rose and
fell like something taking deep, happy breaths;
and the sound was musical, seemed to come from
the throat of spring. Not far away, on the corner, was an old man selling English violets, each
bunch wrapped in oiled paper to protect them
from the snow. Here, I felt, winter brought no
desolation; it was tamed, like a polar bear led on
a leash by a beautiful lady.

About the Square the pale blue shadows grew
denser and drew closer. The street lamps flashed
out all along the Avenue, and soft lights began to
twinkle in the tall buildings while it was yet day

—violet buildings, just a little denser in sub-
stance and colour than the violet sky. While I
was gazing up at them I heard a laugh close beside me, and Mrs. Henshawe's arm slipped
through mine.

"Why, you're fair moon-struck, Nellie! I've
seen the messenger boys dodging all about you!"
It was true, droves of people were going through
the Square now, and boys carrying potted plants
and big wreaths. "Don't you like to watch them?
But we can't stay. We're going home to Oswald.
Oh, hear the penny whistle! They always find
me out." She stopped a thin lad with a cap and
yarn comforter but no overcoat, who was playing
The Irish Washerwoman on a little pipe, and
rummaged in her bag for a coin.

The Henshawes' apartment was the second
floor of an old brownstone house on the north side
of the Square. I loved it from the moment I entered it; such solidly built, high-ceiled rooms,
with snug fire-places and wide doors and deep
windows. The long, heavy velvet curtains and
the velvet chairs were a wonderful plum-colour,
like ripe purple fruit. The curtains were lined

with that rich cream-colour that lies under the blue skin of ripe figs.

Oswald was standing by the fire, drinking a whisky and soda while he waited for us. He put his glass down on the mantel as we opened the door, and forgot all about it. He pushed chairs up to the hearth for my aunt and me, and stood talking to us while his wife went to change her dress and to have a word with the Irish maid before dinner.

"By the way, Myra," he said, as she left us, "I've put a bottle of champagne on ice; it's Christmas eve."

Everything in their little apartment seemed to me absolutely individual and unique, even the dinner service; the thick grey plates and the soup tureen painted with birds and big, bright flowers —I was sure there were no others like them in the world.

As we were finishing dinner the maid announced Mr. Gray. Henshawe went into the parlour to greet him, and we followed a moment later. The young man was in evening clothes, with a few sprays of white hyacinth in his coat.

He stood by the fire, his arm on the mantel. His clean, fair skin and melancholy eyes, his very correct clothes, and something about the shape of his hands, made one conscious of a cool, deliberate fastidiousness in him. In spite of his spotty past he looked, that night, as fresh and undamaged as the flowers he wore. Henshawe took on a slightly bantering tone with him, and seemed to be trying to cheer him up. Mr. Gray would not sit down. After an interval of polite conversation he said to his host: "Will you excuse me if I take Myra away for a few moments? She has promised to do something kind for me."

They went into Henshawe's little study, off the parlour, and shut the door. We could hear a low murmur of voices. When they came back to us Mrs. Henshawe stood beside Gray while he put on his caped cloak, talking encouragingly. "The opals are beautiful, but I'm afraid of them, Ewan. Oswald would laugh at me, but all the same they have a bad history. Love itself draws on a woman nearly all the bad luck in the world; why, for mercy's sake, add opals? He brought two bracelets for me to decide between them,

Oswald, both lovely. However did they let you carry off two, Ewan?"

"They know me there. I always pay my bills, Myra. I don't know why, but I do. I suppose it's the Scotch in me."

He wished us all good-night.

"Give a kiss to Esther for me," said Mrs. Henshawe merrily at the door. He made no reply, but bent over her hand and vanished.

"What he really wanted was to show me some verses he's made for her," said Mrs. Henshawe, as she came back to the fire. "And very pretty ones they are, for sweet-heart poetry."

Mr. Henshawe smiled. "Maybe you obliged him with a rhyme or two, my dear? Lydia—" he sat down by my aunt and put his hand on hers— "I'd never feel sure that I did my own courting, if it weren't that I was a long way off at the time. Myra is so fond of helping young men along. We nearly always have a love affair on hand."

She put her hand over his lips. "Hush! I hate old women who egg on courtships."

When Oswald had finished his cigar we were taken out for a walk. This was primarily for the good of her "figger," Myra said, and incidentally we were to look for a green bush to send to Madame Modjeska. "She's spending the holidays in town, and it will be dismal at her hotel."

At the florist's we found, among all the little trees and potted plants, a glistening holly-tree, full of red berries and pointed like a spire, easily the queen of its companions. "That is naturally hers," said Mrs. Myra.

Her husband shrugged. "It's naturally the most extravagant."

Mrs. Myra threw up her head. "Don't be petty, Oswald. It's not a woollen petticoat or warm mittens that Madame is needing." She gave careful instructions to the florist's man, who was to take the tree to the Savoy; he was to carry with it a box of cakes, "of my baking," she said proudly. He was to ask for Mrs. Hewes, the housekeeper, and under her guidance he was to carry the tree up to Madame Modjeska's rooms himself. The man showed a sympathetic interest, and promised to follow instructions. Then Mrs. Henshawe gave him a silver dollar and wished him a Merry Christmas.

As we walked home she slipped her arm through mine, and we fell a little behind the other two. "See the moon coming out, Nellie— behind the tower. It wakens the guilt in me. No playing with love; and I'd sworn a great oath never to meddle again. You send a handsome fellow like Ewan Gray to a fine girl like Esther, and it's Christmas eve, and they rise above us and the white world around us, and there isn't anybody, not a tramp on the park benches, that wouldn't wish them well—and very likely hell will come of it!"

4

THE NEXT morning Oswald Henshawe, in a frock-coat and top-hat, called to take Aunt Lydia and me to church. The weather had cleared before we went to bed, and as we stepped out of our hotel that morning, the sun shone blindingly on the snow-covered park, the gold Diana flashed against a green-blue sky. We were going to Grace Church, and the morning was so beautiful that we decided to walk.

"Lydia," said Henshawe, as he took us each

by an arm, "I want you to give me a Christmas present."

"Why, Oswald," she stammered.

"Oh, I have it ready! You've only to present it." He took a little flat package from his pocket and slipped it into her muff. He drew both of us closer to him. "Listen, it's nothing. It's some sleeve-buttons, given me by a young woman who means no harm, but doesn't know the ways of the world very well. She's from a breezy Western city, where a rich girl can give a present whenever she wants to and nobody questions it. She sent these to my office yesterday. If I send them back to her it will hurt her feelings; she would think I had misunderstood her. She'll get hard knocks here, of course, but I don't want to give her any. On the other hand—well, you know Myra; nobody better. She would punish herself and everybody else for this young woman's questionable taste. So I want you to give them to me, Lydia."

"Oh, Oswald," cried my aunt, "Myra is so keen! I'm not clever enough to fool Myra. Can't you just put them away in your office?"

"Not very well. Besides," he gave a slightly

embarrassed laugh, "I'd like to wear them. They are very pretty."

"Now, Oswald . . ."

"Oh, it's all right, Lydia, I give you my word it is. But you know how a little thing of that sort can upset my wife. I thought you might give them to me when you come over to dine with us to-morrow night. She wouldn't be jealous of you. But if you don't like the idea . . . why, just take them home with you and give them to some nice boy who would appreciate them."

All through the Christmas service I could see that Aunt Lydia was distracted and perplexed. As soon as we got back to the hotel and were safe in our rooms she took the brown leather case from her muff and opened it. The sleeve-buttons were topazes, winy-yellow, lightly set in crinkly gold. I believe she was seduced by their beauty. "I really think he ought to have them, if he wants them. Everything is always for Myra. He never gets anything for himself. And all the admiration is for her; why shouldn't he have a little? He has been devoted to a fault. It isn't good for any woman to be humoured and pampered as he has humoured her. And she's often most unreasonable with him—most unreasonable!"

The next evening, as we were walking across the Square to the Henshawes, we glanced up and saw them standing together in one of their deep front windows, framed by the plum-coloured curtains. They were looking out, but did not see us. I noticed that she was really quite a head shorter than he, and she leaned a little towards him. When she was peaceful, she was like a dove with its wings folded. There was something about them, as they stood in the lighted window, that would have discouraged me from meddling, but it did not shake my aunt.

As soon as we were in the parlour, before we had taken off our coats, she said resolutely: "Myra, I want to give Oswald a Christmas present. Once an old friend left with me some cufflinks he couldn't keep—unpleasant associations, I suppose. I thought of giving them to one of my own boys, but I brought them for Oswald. I'd rather he would have them than anybody."

Aunt Lydia spoke with an ease and conviction which compelled my admiration. She took

the buttons out of her muff, without the box, of
course, and laid them in Mrs. Henshawe's hand.

Mrs. Henshawe was delighted. "How clever
of you to think of it, Liddy, dear! Yes, they're
exactly right for him. There's hardly any other
stone I would like, but these are exactly right.
Look, Oswald, they're the colour of a fine Mo-
selle." It was Oswald himself who seemed disturbed, and not overpleased. He grew red, was
confused in his remarks, and was genuinely reluctant when his wife insisted upon taking the
gold buttons out of his cuffs and putting in the
new ones. "I can't get over your canniness,
Liddy," she said as she fitted them.

"It's not like me, is it, Myra?" retorted my
aunt; "not like me at all to choose the right sort
of thing. But did it never occur to you that anyone besides yourself might know what is appro-
priate for Oswald? No, I'm sure it never did!"

Mrs. Myra took the laugh so heartily to herself that I felt it was a shame to deceive her. So,
I am sure, did Oswald. During dinner he talked
more than usual, but he was ill at ease. Afterwards, at the opera, when the lights were down, I

noticed that he was not listening to the music, but was looking listlessly off into the gloom of the house, with something almost sorrowful in his strange, half-moon eyes. During an *entr'acte* a door at the back was opened, and a draught blew in. As he put his arm back to pull up the cloak which had slipped down from his wife's bare shoulders, she laughed and said: "Oh, Oswald, I love to see your jewels flash!"

He dropped his hand quickly and frowned so darkly that I thought he would have liked to put the topazes under his heel and grind them up. I thought him properly served then, but often since I have wondered at his gentle heart.

5

DURING the week between Christmas and New Year's day I was with Mrs. Henshawe a great deal, but we were seldom alone. It was the season of calls and visits, and she said that meeting so many people would certainly improve my manners and my English. She hated my careless, slangy, Western speech. Her friends, I found, were of two kinds: artistic people—actors, musicians, literary men—with whom she was always at her best because she admired them; and another group whom she called her "moneyed" friends (she seemed to like the word), and these she cultivated, she told me, on Oswald's account. "He is the sort of man who does well in business only if he has the incentive of friendships. He doesn't properly belong in business. We never speak of it, but I'm sure he hates it. He went into an office only because we were young and terribly in love, and had to be married."

The business friends seemed to be nearly all Germans. On Sunday we called at half-a-dozen or more big houses. I remember very large rooms, much upholstered and furnished, walls hung with large paintings in massive frames, and many stiff, dumpy little sofas, in which the women sat two-and-two, while the men stood about the refreshment tables, drinking champagne and coffee and smoking fat black cigars. Among these people Mrs. Myra took on her loftiest and most challenging manner. I could see that some of the women were quite afraid of her. They were in great haste to rush refreshments to her, and looked troubled when she refused anything. They addressed her in German and profusely complimented her upon the way she spoke it. We had a carriage that afternoon, and Myra was dressed in her best —making an especial effort on Oswald's account; but the rich and powerful irritated her. Their solemnity was too much for her sense of humour; there was a biting edge to her sarcasm, a curl about the corners of her mouth that was never there when she was with people whose personality charmed her.

I had one long, delightful afternoon alone with Mrs. Henshawe in Central Park. We walked for miles, stopped to watch the skating, and finally had tea at the Casino, where she told me about some of the singers and actors I would meet at her apartment on New Year's eve. Her account of her friends was often more interesting to me than the people themselves. After tea she hailed a hansom and asked the man to drive us about the park a little, as a fine sunset was coming on. We were jogging happily along under the elms, watching the light change on the crusted snow, when a carriage passed from which a handsome woman leaned out and waved to us. Mrs. Henshawe bowed stiffly, with a condescending smile.

"There, Nellie," she exclaimed, "that's the last woman I'd care to have splashing past me, and me in a hansom cab!"

I glimpsed what seemed to me insane ambition. My aunt was always thanking God that the Henshawes got along as well as they did, and worrying because she felt sure Oswald wasn't saving anything. And here Mrs. Myra was wishing for a carriage—with stables and a house and servants, and all that went with a carriage! All the way home she kept her scornful expression, holding her head high and sniffing the purple air from side to side as we drove down Fifth Avenue. When we alighted before her door she paid the driver, and gave him such a large fee that he snatched off his hat and said twice: "Thank you, thank you, my lady!" She dismissed him with a smile and a nod. "All the same," she whispered to me as she fitted her latchkey, "it's very nasty, being poor!"

That week Mrs. Henshawe took me to see a dear friend of hers, Anne Aylward, the poet. She was a girl who had come to New York only a few years before, had won the admiration of men of letters, and was now dying of tuberculosis in her early twenties. Mrs. Henshawe had given me a book of her poems to read, saying: "I want you to see her so that you can remember her in after years, and I want her to see you so that we can talk you over."

Miss Aylward lived with her mother in a small flat overlooking the East River, and we found her in a bathchair, lying in the sun and watching the river boats go by. Her study was a delightful place that morning, full of flowers and plants and baskets of fruit that had been sent her for Christmas. But it was Myra Henshawe herself who made that visit so memorably gay. Never had I seen her so brilliant and strangely charming as she was in that sunlit study up under the roofs. Their talk quite took my breath away; they said such exciting, such fantastic things about people, books, music—anything; they seemed to speak together a kind of highly flavoured special language.

As we were walking home she tried to tell me more about Miss Aylward, but tenderness for her friend and bitter rebellion at her fate choked her voice. She suffered physical anguish for that poor girl. My aunt often said that Myra was incorrigibly extravagant; but I saw that her chief extravagance was in caring for so many people and in caring for them so much. When she but mentioned the name of someone whom she admired, one got an instant impression that the person must be wonderful, her voice invested the name with a sort of grace. When she liked people she always called them by name a great many times in talking to them, and she enunciated the name, no matter how commonplace, in a penetrating way, without hurrying over it or slurring it; and this, accompanied by her singularly direct glance, had a curious effect. When she addressed Aunt Lydia, for instance, she seemed to be speaking to a person deeper down than the blurred, taken-for-granted image of my aunt that I saw every day, and for a moment my aunt became more individual, less matter-of-fact to me. I had noticed this peculiar effect of Myra's look and vocative when I first met her, in Parthia, where her manner of addressing my relatives had made them all seem a little more attractive to me.

One afternoon when we were at a matinée I noticed in a loge a young man who looked very much like the photographs of a story-writer popular at that time. I asked Mrs. Henshawe whether it could be he. She looked in the direction I indicated, then looked quickly away again.

"Yes, it's he. He used to be a friend of mine. That's a sad phrase, isn't it? But there was a time when he could have stood by Oswald in a difficulty—and he didn't. He passed it up. Wasn't there. I've never forgiven him."

I regretted having noticed the man in the loge, for all the rest of the afternoon I could feel the bitterness working in her. I knew that she was suffering. The scene on the stage was obliterated for her; the drama was in her mind. She was going over it all again; arguing, accusing, denouncing.

As we left the theatre she sighed: "Oh, Nellie, I wish you hadn't seen him! It's all very well to tell us to forgive our enemies; our enemies can never hurt us very much. But oh, what about forgiving our friends?"—she beat on her fur collar with her two gloved hands—"that's where the rub comes!"

The Henshawes always gave a party on New Year's eve. That year most of the guests were stage people. Some of them, in order to get there before midnight, came with traces of make-up still on their faces. I remember old Jefferson de Angelais arrived in his last-act wig, carrying his plumed hat—during the supper his painted eyebrows spread and came down over his eyes like a veil. Most of them are dead now, but it was a fine group that stood about the table to drink the New Year in. By far the handsomest and most distinguished of that company was a woman no longer young, but beautiful in age, Helena Modjeska. She looked a woman of another race and another period, no less queenly than when I had seen her in Chicago as Marie Stuart, and as Katharine in *Henry VIII*. I remember how, when Oswald asked her to propose a toast, she put out her long arm, lifted her glass, and looking into the blur of the candlelight with a grave face, said: "To my coun-n-try!"

As she was not playing, she had come early,

some time before the others, bringing with her a young Polish woman who was singing at the Opera that winter. I had an opportunity to watch Modjeska as she sat talking to Myra and Esther Sinclair—Miss Sinclair had once played in her company. When the other guests began to arrive, and Myra was called away, she sat by the fire in a high-backed chair, her head resting lightly on her hand, her beautiful face half in shadow. How well I remember those long, beautifully modelled hands, with so much humanity in them. They were worldly, indeed, but fashioned for a nobler worldliness than ours; hands to hold a sceptre, or a chalice—or, by courtesy, a sword.

The party did not last long, but it was a whirl of high spirits. Everybody was hungry and thirsty. There was a great deal of talk about Sarah Bernhardt's *Hamlet*, which had been running all week and had aroused hot controversy; and about Jean de Reszke's return to the Metropolitan that night, after a long illness in London.

By two o'clock everyone had gone but the two Polish ladies. Modjeska, after she put on her long cloak, went to the window, drew back the plum-coloured curtains, and looked out. "See, Myra," she said with that Slav accent she never lost, though she read English verse so beautifully, "the Square is quite white with moonlight. And how still all the ci-ty is, how still!" She turned to her friend; "Emelia, I think you must sing something. Something old . . . yes, from *Norma*." She hummed a familiar air under her breath, and looked about for a chair. Oswald brought one. "Thank you. And we might have less light, might we not?" He turned off the lights.

She sat by the window, half draped in her cloak, the moonlight falling across her knees. Her friend went to the piano and commenced the *Casta Diva* aria, which begins so like the quivering of moonbeams on the water. It was the first air on our old music-box at home, but I had never heard it sung—and I have never heard it sung so beautifully since. I remember Oswald, standing like a statue behind Madame Modjeska's chair, and Myra, crouching low beside the singer, her head in both hands, while the song grew and blossomed like a great emotion.

When it stopped, nobody said anything beyond a low good-bye. Modjeska again drew her cloak around her, and Oswald took them down to their carriage. Aunt Lydia and I followed, and as we crossed the Square we saw their cab going up the Avenue. For many years I associated Mrs. Henshawe with that music, thought of that aria as being mysteriously related to something in her nature that one rarely saw, but nearly always felt; a compelling, passionate, overmastering something for which I had no name, but which was audible, visible in the air that night, as she sat crouching in the shadow. When I wanted to recall powerfully that hidden richness in her, I had only to close my eyes and sing to myself: *"Casta diva, casta diva!"*

6

ON SATURDAY I was to lunch at the Henshawes' and go alone with Oswald to hear Bernhardt and Coquelin. As I opened the door into the entry hall, the first thing that greeted me was Mrs. Henshawe's angry laugh, and a burst of rapid words that stung like cold water from a spray.

"I tell you, I will know the truth about this key, and I will go through any door your keys open. Is that clear?"

Oswald answered with a distinctly malicious chuckle: "My dear, you'd have a hard time getting through that door. The key happens to open a safety deposit box."

Her voice rose an octave in pitch. "How dare you lie to me, Oswald? How dare you? They told me at your bank that this wasn't a bank key, though it looks like one. I stopped and showed it to them—the day you forgot your keys and telephoned me to bring them down to your office."

"The hell you did!"

I coughed and rapped at the door . . . they took no notice of me. I heard Oswald push back a chair. "Then it was you who took my keys out of my pocket? I might have known it! I never forget to change them. And you went to the bank and made me and yourself ridiculous. I can imagine their amusement."

"Well, you needn't! I know how to get information without giving any. Here is Nellie Birdseye, rapping at the gates. Come in, Nellie. You and Oswald are going over to Martin's for lunch. He and I are quarrelling about a key ring. There will be no luncheon here to-day."

She went away, and I stood bewildered. This delightful room had seemed to me a place where light-heartedness and charming manners lived— housed there just as the purple curtains and the Kiva rugs and the gay water-colours were. And now everything was in ruins. The air was still and cold like the air in a refrigerating-room. What I felt was fear; I was afraid to look or speak or move. Everything about me seemed evil. When kindness has left people, even for a few moments, we become afraid of them, as if their reason had left them. When it has left a place where we have always found it, it is like ship-wreck; we drop from security into something malevolent and bottomless.

"It's all right, Nellie." Oswald recovered himself and put a hand on my shoulder. "Myra isn't half so furious with me as she pretends. I'll get my hat and we'll be off." He was in his smoking-jacket, and had been sitting at his desk, writing. His inkwell was uncovered, and on the blotter lay a half-written sheet of note paper.

I was glad to get out into the sunlight with him. The city seemed safe and friendly and smiling.

The air in that room had been like poison. Oswald tried to make it up to me. We walked round and round the Square, and at Martin's he made me drink a glass of sherry, and pointed out the interesting people in the dining-room and told me stories about them. But without his hat, his head against the bright window, he looked tired and troubled. I wondered, as on the first time I saw him, in my own town, at the contradiction in his face: the strong bones, and the curiously shaped eyes without any fire in them. I felt that his life had not suited him; that he possessed some kind of courage and force which slept, which in another sort of world might have asserted themselves brilliantly. I thought he ought to have been a soldier or an explorer. I have since seen those half-moon eyes in other people, and they were always inscrutable, like his; fronted the world with courtesy and kindness, but one never got behind them.

We went to the theatre, but I remember very little of the performance except a dull heartache, and a conviction that I should never like Mrs. Myra so well again. That was on Saturday. On

Monday Aunt Lydia and I were to start for home. We positively did not see the Henshawes again. Sunday morning the maid came with some flowers and a note from Myra, saying that her friend Anne Aylward was having a bad day and had sent for her.

On Monday we took an early boat across the ferry, in order to breakfast in the Jersey station before our train started. We had got settled in our places in the Pullman, the moment of departure was near, when we heard an amused laugh, and there was Myra Henshawe, coming into the car in her fur hat, followed by a porter who carried her bags.

"I didn't plot anything so neat as this, Liddy," she laughed, a little out of breath, "though I knew we'd be on the same train. But we won't quarrel, will we? I'm only going as far as Pittsburgh. I've some old friends there. Oswald and I have had a disagreement, and I've left him to think it over. If he needs me, he can quite well come after me."

All day Mrs. Myra was jolly and agreeable, though she treated us with light formality, as if we were new acquaintances. We lunched together, and I noticed, sitting opposite her, that when she was in this mood of high scorn, her mouth, which could be so tender—which cherished the names of her friends and spoke them delicately—was entirely different. It seemed to curl and twist about like a little snake. Letting herself think harm of anyone she loved seemed to change her nature, even her features.

It was dark when we got into Pittsburgh. The Pullman porter took Myra's luggage to the end of the car. She bade us good-bye, started to leave us, then turned back with an icy little smile. "Oh, Liddy dear, you needn't have perjured yourself for those yellow cuff-buttons. I was sure to find out, I always do. I don't hold it against you, but it's disgusting in a man to lie for personal decorations. A woman might do it, now, . . . for pearls!" With a bright nod she turned away and swept out of the car, her head high, the long garnet feather drooping behind.

Aunt Lydia was very angry. "I'm sick of Myra's dramatics," she declared. "I've done with them. A man never *is* justified, but if ever a man was . . ."

PART

II

I

Ten years after that visit to New York I happened to be in a sprawling overgrown West-coast city which was in the throes of rapid development—it ran about the shore, stumbling all over itself and finally tumbled untidily into the sea. Every hotel and boarding-house was overcrowded, and I was very poor. Things had gone badly with my family and with me. I had come West in the middle of the year to take a position in a college—a college that was as experimental and unsubstantial as everything else in the place. I found lodgings in an apartment-hotel, wretchedly built and already falling to pieces, although it was new. I moved in on a Sunday morning, and while I was unpacking my trunk, I heard, through the thin walls, my neighbour stirring about; a man, and, from the huskiness of his cough and something measured in his movements, not a young man. The caution of his step, the guarded consideration of his activities, let me know that he did not wish to thrust the details of his housekeeping upon other people any more than he could help.

Presently I detected the ugly smell of gasolene in the air, heard a sound of silk being snapped and shaken, and then a voice humming very low an old German air—yes, Schubert's *Frühlingsglaube*; ta ta te–ta | ta–ta ta–ta ta–ta | ta. In a moment I saw the ends of dark neckties fluttering out of the window next mine.

All this made me melancholy—more than the dreariness of my own case. I was young, and it didn't matter so much about me; for youth there is always the hope, the certainty, of better things.

But an old man, a gentleman, living in this shabby, comfortless place, cleaning his neckties of a Sunday morning and humming to himself . . . it depressed me unreasonably. I was glad when his outer door shut softly and I heard no more of him.

There was an indifferent restaurant on the ground floor of the hotel. As I was going down to my dinner that evening, I met, at the head of the stairs, a man coming up and carrying a large black tin tray. His head was bent, and his eyes were lowered. As he drew aside to let me pass, in spite of his thin white hair and stooped shoulders, I recognised Oswald Henshawe, whom I had not seen for so many years—not, indeed, since that afternoon when he took me to see Sarah Bernhardt play *Hamlet*.

When I called his name he started, looked at me, and rested the tray on the sill of the blindless window that lighted the naked stairway.

"Nellie! Nellie Birdseye! Can it be?"

His voice was quite uncertain. He seemed deeply shaken, and pulled out a handkerchief to wipe his forehead. "But, Nellie, you have grown up! I would not know you. What good fortune for Myra! She will hardly believe it when I tell her. She is ill, my poor Myra. Oh, very ill! But we must not speak of that, nor seem to know it. What it will mean to her to see you again! Her friends always were so much to her, you remember? Will you stop and see us as you come up? Her room is thirty-two; rap gently, and I'll be waiting for you. Now I must take her dinner. Oh, I hope for her sake you are staying some time. She has no one here."

He took up the tray and went softly along the uncarpeted hall. I felt little zest for the canned vegetables and hard meat the waitress put before me. I had known that the Henshawes had come on evil days, and were wandering about among the cities of the Pacific coast. But Myra had stopped writing to Aunt Lydia, beyond a word of greeting at Christmas and on her birthday. She had ceased to give us any information about their way of life. We knew that several years after my memorable visit in New York, the railroad to whose president Oswald had long been private secretary, was put into the hands of a receiver, and the retiring president went abroad to live. Henshawe had remained with the new management, but very soon the road was taken over by one of the great trunk lines, and the office staff was cut in two. In the reorganization Henshawe was offered a small position, which he indignantly refused—his wife wouldn't let him think of accepting it. He went to San Francisco as manager of a commission house; the business failed, and what had happened to them since I did not know.

I lingered long over my dismal dinner. I had not the courage to go upstairs. Henshawe was not more than sixty, but he looked much older. He had the tired, tired face of one who has utterly lost hope.

Oswald had got his wife up out of bed to receive me. When I entered she was sitting in a wheel-chair by an open window, wrapped in a Chinese dressing-gown, with a bright shawl over her feet. She threw out both arms to me, and as she hugged me, flashed into her old gay laugh.

"Now wasn't it clever of you to find us, Nellie? And we so safely hidden—in earth, like a pair of old foxes! But it was in the cards that we should meet again. Now I understand; a wise woman has been coming to read my fortune for me, and the queen of hearts has been coming up out of the pack when she had no business to; a beloved friend coming out of the past. Well, Nellie, dear, I couldn't think of any old friends that weren't better away, for one reason or another, while we are in temporary eclipse. I gain strength faster if I haven't people on my mind. But you, Nellie . . . that's different." She put my two hands to her cheeks, making a frame for her face. "That's different. Somebody young, and clear-eyed, chock-full of opinions, and without a past. But you may have a past, already? The darkest ones come early."

I was delighted. She was . . . she was herself, Myra Henshawe! I hadn't expected anything so good. The electric bulbs in the room were shrouded and muffled with coloured scarfs, and in that light she looked much less changed than Oswald. The corners of her mouth had relaxed a little, but they could still curl very scornfully upon occasion; her nose was the same sniffy

little nose, with its restless, arched nostrils, and
her double chin, though softer, was no fuller. A
strong cable of grey-black hair was wound on the
top of her head, which, as she once remarked,
"was no head for a woman at all, but would have
graced one of the wickedest of the Roman em-
perors."

Her bed was in the alcove behind her. In the
shadowy dimness of the room I recognised some
of the rugs from their New York apartment,
some of the old pictures, with frames peeling and
glass cracked. Here was Myra's little inlaid tea-
table, and the desk at which Oswald had been
writing that day when I dropped in upon their
quarrel. At the windows were the dear, plum-
coloured curtains, their cream lining streaked
and faded—but the sight of them rejoiced me
more than I could tell the Henshawes.

"And where did you come from, Nellie?
What are you doing here, in heaven's name?"

While I explained myself she listened intently,
holding my wrist with one of her beautiful little
hands, which were so inexplicably mischievous

in their outline, and which, I noticed, were still white and well cared for.

"Ah, but teaching, Nellie! I don't like that, not even for a temporary expedient. It's a cul-de-sac. Generous young people use themselves all up at it; they have no sense. Only the stupid and the phlegmatic should teach."

"But won't you allow me, too, a temporary eclipse?"

She laughed and squeezed my hand. "Ah, we wouldn't be hiding in the shadow, if we were five-and-twenty! We were throwing off sparks like a pair of shooting stars, weren't we, Oswald? No, I can't bear teaching for you, Nellie. Why not journalism? You could always make your way easily there."

"Because I hate journalism. I know what I want to do, and I'll work my way out yet, if only you'll give me time."

"Very well, dear." She sighed. "But I'm ambitious for you. I've no patience with young people when they drift. I wish I could live their lives for them; I'd know how! But there it is; by the time you've learned the short cuts, your feet puff up so that you can't take the road at all. Now tell me about your mother and my Lydia."

I had hardly begun when she lifted one finger and sniffed the air. "Do you get it? That bitter smell of the sea? It's apt to come in on the night wind. I live on it. Sometimes I can still take a drive along the shore. Go on; you say that Lydia and your mother are at present in disputation about the possession of your late grandfather's portrait. Why don't you cut it in two for them, Nellie? I remember it perfectly, and half of it would be enough for anybody!"

While I told her any amusing gossip I could remember about my family, she sat crippled but powerful in her brilliant wrappings. She looked strong and broken, generous and tyrannical, a witty and rather wicked old woman, who hated life for its defeats, and loved it for its absurdities. I recalled her angry laugh, and how she had always greeted shock or sorrow with that dry, exultant chuckle which seemed to say: "Ah-ha, I have one more piece of evidence, one more, against the hideous injustice God permits in this world!"

While we were talking, the silence of the strangely balmy February evening was rudely disturbed by the sound of doors slamming and heavy tramping overhead. Mrs. Henshawe winced, a look of apprehension and helplessness, a tortured expression, came over her face. She turned sharply to her husband, who was resting peacefully in one of their old, deep chairs, over by the muffled light. "There they are, those animals!"

He sat up. "They have just come back from church," he said in a troubled voice.

"Why should I have to know when they come back from church? Why should I have the details of their stupid, messy existence thrust upon me all day long, and half the night?" she broke out bitterly. Her features became tense, as from an attack of pain, and I realised how unable she was to bear things.

"We are unfortunate in the people who live over us," Oswald explained. "They annoy us a great deal. These new houses are poorly built, and every sound carries."

"Couldn't you ask them to walk more quietly?" I suggested.

He smiled and shook his head. "We have, but it seems to make them worse. They are that kind of people."

His wife broke in. "The palavery kind of Southerners; all that slushy gush on the surface, and no sensibilities whatever—a race without consonants and without delicacy. They tramp up there all day long like cattle. The stalled ox would have trod softer. Their energy isn't worth anything, so they use it up gabbling and running about, beating my brains into a jelly."

She had scarcely stopped for breath when I heard a telephone ring overhead, then shrieks of laughter, and two people ran across the floor as if they were running a foot-race.

"You hear?" Mrs. Henshawe looked at me triumphantly. "Those two silly old hens race each other to the telephone as if they had a sweetheart at the other end of it. While I could still climb stairs, I hobbled up to that woman and implored her, and she began gushing about 'mah sistah' and 'mah son,' and what 'rahfined' people they were. . . . Oh, that's the cruelty of being poor; it leaves you at the mercy of such pigs! Money is a protection, a cloak; it can buy one quiet, and some sort of dignity." She leaned back, exhausted, and shut her eyes.

"Come, Nellie," said Oswald, softly. He walked down the hall to my door with me. "I'm sorry the disturbance began while you were there. Sometimes they go to the movies, and stay out later," he said mournfully. "I've talked to that woman and to her son, but they are very unfeeling people."

"But wouldn't the management interfere in a case of sickness?"

Again he shook his head. "No, they pay a higher rent than we do—occupy more rooms. And we are somewhat under obligation to the management."

2

I soon discovered the facts about the Henshawes' present existence. Oswald had a humble position, poorly paid, with the city traction company. He had to be at his desk at nine o'clock every day except Sunday. He rose at five in the morning, put on an old duck suit (it happened to be a very smart one, with frogs and a military collar, left over from prosperous times), went to his wife's room and gave her her bath, made her bed, arranged her things, and then got their breakfast. He made the coffee on a spirit lamp, the toast on an electric toaster. This was the only meal of the day they could have together, and as they had it long before the ruthless Poindexters overhead began to tramp, it was usually a cheerful occasion.

After breakfast Oswald washed the dishes. Their one luxury was a private bath, with a large cupboard, which he called his kitchen. Everything else done, he went back to his own room, put it in order, and then dressed for the office. He still dressed very neatly, though how he managed to do it with the few clothes he had, I could not see. He was the only man staying in that shabby hotel who looked well-groomed. As a special favour from his company he was allowed to take two hours at noon, on account of his sick wife. He came home, brought her her lunch from below, then hurried back to his office.

Myra made her own tea every afternoon, getting about in her wheel-chair or with the aid of a cane. I found that one of the kindest things I could do for her was to bring her some little sandwiches or cakes from the Swedish bakery to vary her tinned biscuit. She took great pains to get her tea nicely; it made her feel less shabby to use her own silver tea things and the three glossy English cups she had carried about with her in her trunk. I used often to go in and join her, and we spent some of our pleasantest hours at that time of the day, when the people overhead were usually out. When they were in, and active, it was too painful to witness Mrs. Henshawe's suffering. She was acutely sensitive to sound and light, and the Poindexters did tramp like cattle—except that their brutal thumping hadn't the measured dignity which the step of animals always has. Mrs. Henshawe got great pleasure from flowers, too, and during the late winter months my chief extravagance and my chief pleasure was in taking them to her.

One warm Saturday afternoon, early in April, we went for a drive along the shore. I had hired a low carriage with a kindly Negro driver. Supported on his arm and mine, Mrs. Henshawe managed to get downstairs. She looked much older and more ill in her black broadcloth coat and a black taffeta hat that had once been smart.

We took with us her furs and an old steamer blanket. It was a beautiful, soft spring day. The road, unfortunately, kept winding away from the sea. At last we came out on a bare headland, with only one old twisted tree upon it, and the sea beneath.

"Why, Nellie!" she exclaimed, "it's like the cliff in *Lear*, Gloucester's cliff, so it is! Can't we stay here? I believe this nice darkey man would fix me up under the tree there and come back for us later."

We wrapped her in the rug, and she declared that the trunk of the old cedar, bending away from the sea, made a comfortable back for her. The Negro drove away, and I went for a walk up the shore because I knew she wanted to be alone. From a distance I could see her leaning against her tree and looking off to sea, as if she were waiting for something. A few steamers passed below her, and the gulls dipped and darted about the headland, the soft shine of the sun on their wings. The afternoon light, at first wide and watery-pale, grew stronger and yellower, and when I went back to Myra it was beating from the west on her cliff as if thrown by a burning-glass.

She looked up at me with a soft smile—her face could still be very lovely in a tender moment. "I've had such a beautiful hour, dear; or has it been longer? Light and silence: they heal all one's wounds—all but one, and that is healed by dark and silence. I find I don't miss clever talk, the kind I always used to have about me, when I can have silence. It's like cold water poured over fever."

I sat down beside her, and we watched the sun dropping lower toward his final plunge into the Pacific. "I'd love to see this place at dawn," Myra said suddenly. "That is always such a forgiving time. When that first cold, bright streak comes over the water, it's as if all our sins were pardoned; as if the sky leaned over the earth and kissed it and gave it absolution. You know how the great sinners always came home to die in some religious house, and the abbot or the abbess went out and received them with a kiss?"

When we got home she was, of course, very tired. Oswald was waiting for us, and he and the driver carried her upstairs. While we were getting her into bed, the noise overhead broke out —tramp, tramp, bang! Myra began to cry.

"Oh, I've come back to it, to be tormented again! I've two fatal maladies, but it's those coarse creatures I shall die of. Why didn't you leave me out there, Nellie, in the wind and night? You ought to get me away from this, Oswald. If I were on my feet, and you laid low, I wouldn't let you be despised and trampled upon."

"I'll go up and see those people to-morrow, Mrs. Henshawe," I promised. "I'm sure I can do something."

"Oh, don't, Nellie!" She looked up at me in affright. "She'd turn a deaf ear to you. You know the Bible says the wicked are deaf like the adder. And, Nellie, she has the wrinkled, white throat of an adder, that woman, and the hard eyes of one. Don't go near her!"

(I went to see Mrs. Poindexter the next day, and she had just such a throat and just such eyes. She smiled, and said that the sick woman underneath was an old story, and she ought to have been sent to a sanatorium long ago.)

"Never mind, Myra. I'll get you away from it yet. I'll manage," Oswald promised as he settled the pillows under her.

She smoothed his hair. "No, my poor Oswald, you'll never stagger far under the bulk of me. Oh, if youth but knew!" She closed her eyes and pressed her hands over them. "It's been the ruin of us both. We've destroyed each other. I should have stayed with my uncle. It was money I needed. We've thrown our lives away."

"Come, Myra, don't talk so before Nellie. You don't mean it. Remember the long time we were happy. That was reality, just as much as this."

"We were never really happy. I am a greedy, selfish, worldly woman; I wanted success and a place in the world. Now I'm old and ill and a fright, but among my own kind I'd still have my circle; I'd have courtesy from people of gentle manners, and not have my brains beaten out by hoodlums. Go away, please, both of you, and leave me!" She turned her face to the wall and covered her head.

We stepped into the hall, and the moment we closed the door we heard the bolt slip behind us.

She must have sprung up very quickly. Oswald walked with me to my room. "It's apt to be like this, when she has enjoyed something and gone beyond her strength. There are times when she can't have anyone near her. It was worse before you came."

I persuaded him to come into my room and sit down and drink a glass of cordial.

"Sometimes she has locked me out for days together," he said. "It seems strange—a woman of such generous friendships. It's as if she had used up that part of herself. It's a great strain on me when she shuts herself up like that. I'm afraid she'll harm herself in some way."

"But people don't do things like that," I said hopelessly.

He smiled and straightened his shoulders. "Ah, but she isn't people! She's Myra Driscoll, and there was never anybody else like her. She can't endure, but she has enough desperate courage for a regiment."

3

THE NEXT morning I saw Henshawe breakfasting in the restaurant, against his custom, so I judged that his wife was still in retreat. I was glad to see that he was not alone, but was talking, with evident pleasure, to a young girl who lived with her mother at this hotel. I had noticed her respectful admiration for Henshawe on other occasions. She worked on a newspaper, was intelligent and, Oswald thought, promising. We enjoyed talking with her at lunch or dinner.

She was perhaps eighteen, overgrown and awkward, with short hair and a rather heavy face; but there was something unusual about her clear, honest eyes that made one wonder. She was always on the watch to catch a moment with Oswald, to get him to talk to her about music, or German poetry, or about the actors and writers he had known. He called her his little chum, and her admiration was undoubtedly a help to him. It was very pretty and naïve. Perhaps that was one of the things that kept him up to the mark in his dress and manner. Among people he never looked apologetic or crushed. He still wore his topaz sleeve-buttons.

On Monday, as I came home from school, I saw that the door of Mrs. Henshawe's room was slightly ajar. She knew my step and called to me: "Can you come in, Nellie?"

She was staying in bed that afternoon, but she had on her best dressing-gown, and she was manicuring her neat little hands—a good sign, I thought.

"Could you stop and have tea with me, and talk? I'll be good to-day, I promise you. I wakened up in the night crying, and it did me good. You see, I was crying about things I never feel now; I'd been dreaming I was young, and the sorrows of youth had set me crying!" She took my hand as I sat down beside her. "Do you know that poem of Heine's, about how he found in his eye a tear that was not of the present, an old one, left over from the kind he used to weep? A tear that belonged to a long dead time of his life and was an anachronism. He couldn't account for it, yet there it was, and he addresses it so prettily: 'Thou old, lonesome tear!' Would you read it for me? There's my little Heine, on the shelf over the sofa. You can easily find the verse, *Du alte, einsame Thräne!*"

I ran through the volume, reading a poem here and there where a leaf had been turned down, or where I saw a line I knew well. It was a fat old book, with yellow pages, bound in tooled leather, and on the fly-leaf, in faint violet ink, was an inscription, "To Myra Driscoll from Oswald," dated 1876.

My friend lay still, with her eyes closed, and occasionally one of those anachronistic tears gathered on her lashes and fell on the pillow, making a little grey spot. Often she took the verse out of my mouth and finished it herself.

"Look for a little short one, about the flower that grows on the suicide's grave, *die Arme-sünderblum'*, the poor-sinner's-flower. Oh, that's the flower for me, Nellie; *die Arme—sünder—blum'!*" She drew the word out until it was a poem in itself.

"Come, dear," she said presently, when I put down the book, "you don't really like this new verse that's going round, ugly lines about ugly people and common feelings—you don't really?"

When I reminded her that she liked Walt Whitman, she chuckled slyly. "Does that save me? Can I get into your new Parnassus on that dirty old man? I suppose I ought to be glad of any sort of ticket at my age! I like naughty rhymes, when they don't try to be pompous. I like the kind bad boys write on fences. My uncle had a rare collection of such rhymes in his head that he'd picked off fences and out-buildings. I wish I'd taken them down; I might become a poet of note! My uncle was a very unusual man. Did they ever tell you much about him at home? Yes, he had violent prejudices; but that's rather good to remember in these days when so few people have any real passions, either of love or hate. He would help a friend, no matter what it cost him, and over and over again he risked ruining himself to crush an enemy. But he never did ruin himself. Men who hate like that usually have the fist-power to back it up, you'll notice. He gave me fair warning, and then he kept his word. I knew he would; we were enough alike for that. He left his money wisely; part of it went to establish a home for aged and destitute women in Chicago, where it was needed."

While we were talking about this institution and some of the refugees it sheltered, Myra said suddenly: "I wonder if you know about a clause concerning me in that foundation? It states that at any time the founder's niece, Myra Driscoll Henshawe, is to be received into the institution, kept without charge, and paid an allowance of ten dollars a week for pocket money until the time of her death. How like the old Satan that was! Be sure when he dictated that provision to

his lawyer, he thought to himself: 'She'd roll herself into the river first, the brach!' And then he
probably thought better of me, and maybe died
with some decent feeling for me in his heart. We
were very proud of each other, and if he'd lived
till now, I'd go back to him and ask his pardon;
because I know what it is to be old and lonely
and disappointed. Yes, and because as we grow
old we become more and more the stuff our fore-
bears put into us. I can feel his savagery
strengthen in me. We think we are so individual
and so misunderstood when we are young; but
the nature our strain of blood carries is inside
there, waiting, like our skeleton."

It had grown quite dusk while we talked.
When I rose and turned on one of the shrouded
lights, Mrs. Henshawe looked up at me and
smiled drolly. "We've had a fine afternoon, and
Biddy forgetting her ails. How the great poets
do shine on, Nellie! Into all the dark corners of
the world. They have no night."

They shone for her, certainly. Miss Stirling,
"a nice young person from the library," as Myra
called her, ran in occasionally with new books,

but Myra's eyes tired quickly, and she used to
shut a new book and lie back and repeat the old
ones she knew by heart, the long declamations
from *Richard II* or *King John*. As I passed her
door I would hear her murmuring at the very
bottom of her rich Irish voice:

Old John of Gaunt, time-honoured Lan-cas-ter . . .

4

ONE AFTERNOON when I got home from school I found a note from Mrs. Henshawe under my door, and went to her at once. She greeted me and kissed me with unusual gravity.

"Nellie, dear, will you do a very special favour for me to-morrow? It is the fifteenth of April, the anniversary of Madame Modjeska's death." She gave me a key and asked me to open an old trunk in the corner. "Lift the tray, and in the bottom, at one end, you will find an old pair of long kid gloves, tied up like sacks. Please give them to me."

I burrowed down under old evening wraps and dinner dresses and came upon the gloves, yellow with age and tied at both ends with corset lacings; they contained something heavy that jingled. Myra was watching my face and chuckled. "Is she thinking they are my wedding gloves, piously preserved? No, my dear; I went before a justice of the peace, and married without gloves, so to speak!" Untying the string, she shook out a little rain of ten- and twenty-dollar gold pieces.

"All old Irish women hide away a bit of money." She took up a coin and gave it to me. "Will you go to St. Joseph's Church and inquire for Father Fay; tell him you are from me, and ask him to celebrate a mass to-morrow for the repose of the soul of Helena Modjeska, Countess Bozenta-Chlapowska. He will remember; last year I hobbled there myself. You are surprised, Nellie? Yes, I broke with the Church when I broke with everything else and ran away with a German free-thinker; but I believe in holy words and holy rites all the same. It is a solace to me to know that to-morrow a mass will will be said here in heathendom for the spirit of that noble artist, that beautiful and gracious woman."

When I put the gold back into the trunk and started making the tea, she said: "Oswald, of course, doesn't know the extent of my resources. We've often needed a hundred dollars or two so bitter bad; he wouldn't understand. But that is money I keep for unearthly purposes; the needs of this world don't touch it."

As I was leaving she called me back: "Oh, Nellie, can't we go to Gloucester's cliff on Saturday, if it's fine? I do long to!"

We went again, and again. Nothing else seemed to give her so much pleasure. But the third time I stopped for her, she declared she was not equal to it. I found her sitting in her chair, trying to write to an old friend, an Irish actress I had met at her apartment in New York, one of the guests at that New York's Eve party. Her son, a young actor, had shot himself in Chicago because of some sordid love affair. I had seen an account of it in the morning paper.

"It touches me very nearly," Mrs. Henshawe

told me. "Why, I used to keep Billy with me for weeks together when his mother was off on tour. He was the most truthful, noble-hearted little fellow. I had so hoped he would be happy. You remember his mother?"

I remembered her very well—large and jovial and hearty she was. Myra began telling me about her, and the son, whom she had not seen since he was sixteen.

"To throw his youth away like that, and shoot himself at twenty-three! People are always talking about the joys of youth—but, oh, how youth can suffer! I've not forgotten; those hot southern Illinois nights, when Oswald was in New York, and I had no word from him except through Liddy, and I used to lie on the floor all night and listen to the express trains go by. I've not forgotten."

"Then I wonder why you are sometimes so hard on him now," I murmured.

Mrs. Henshawe did not reply to me at once. The corners of her mouth trembled, then drew tight, and she sat with her eyes closed as if she were gathering herself for something.

At last she sighed, and looked at me wistfully. "It's a great pity, isn't it, Nellie, to reach out a grudging hand and try to spoil the past for anyone? Yes, it's a great cruelty. But I can't help it. He's a sentimentalist, always was; he can look back on the best of those days when we were young and loved each other, and make himself believe it was all like that. It wasn't. I was always a grasping, worldly woman; I was never satisfied. All the same, in age, when the flowers are so few, it's a great unkindness to destroy any that are left in a man's heart." The tears rolled down her cheeks, she leaned back, looking up at the ceiling. She had stopped speaking because her voice broke. Presently she began again resolutely. "But I'm made so. People can be lovers and enemies at the same time, you know. We were. . . . A man and woman draw apart from that long embrace, and see what they have done to each other. Perhaps I can't forgive him for the harm I did him. Perhaps that's it. When there are children, that feeling goes through natural changes. But when it remains so personal . . .

something gives way in one. In age we lose everything; even the power to love."

"He hasn't," I suggested.

"He has asked you to speak for him, my dear?
Then we have destroyed each other indeed!"

"Certainly he hasn't, Mrs. Myra! But you
are hard on him, you know, and when there are
so many hard things, it seems a pity."

"Yes, it's a great pity." She drew herself up
in her chair. "And I'd rather you didn't come
any more for the time being, Nellie. I've been
thinking the tea made me nervous." She was
smiling, but her mouth curled like a little snake,
as I had seen it do long ago. "Will you be
pleased to take your things and go, Mrs. Casey?"
She said it with a laugh, but a very meaning one.

As I rose I watched for some sign of relenting,
and I said humbly enough: "Forgive me, if I've
said anything I shouldn't. You know I love you
very dearly."

She mockingly bowed her tyrant's head. "It's
owing to me infirmities, dear Mrs. Casey, that
I'll not be able to go as far as me door wid ye."

5

FOR DAYS after that episode I did not see Mrs. Henshawe at all. I saw Oswald at dinner in the restaurant every night, and he reported her condition to me as if nothing had happened. The short-haired newspaper girl often came to our table, and the three of us talked together. I could see that he got great refreshment from her. Her questions woke pleasant trains of recollection, and her straightforward affection was dear to him. Once Myra, in telling me that it was a pleasure to him to have me come into their lives again thus, had remarked: "He was always a man to feel women, you know, in every way." It was true. That crude little girl made all the difference in the world to him. He was generous enough to become quite light-hearted in directing her inexperience and her groping hunger for life. He even read her poor little "specials" and showed her what was worst in them and what was good. She took correction well, he told me.

Early in June Mrs. Henshawe began to grow worse. Her doctors told us a malignant growth in her body had taken hold of a vital organ, and that she would hardly live through the month. She suffered intense pain from pressure on the nerves in her back, and they gave her opiates freely. At first we had two nurses, but Myra hated the night nurse so intensely that we dismissed her, and, as my school was closed for the summer, I took turns with Oswald in watching over her at night. She needed little attention except renewed doses of codeine. She slept deeply for a few hours, and the rest of the night lay awake, murmuring to herself long passages from her old poets.

Myra kept beside her now an ebony crucifix with an ivory Christ. It used to hang on the wall, and I had supposed she carried it about because some friend had given it to her. I felt now that she had it by her for a different reason. Once when I picked it up from her bed to straighten her sheet, she put out her hand quickly and said: "Give it to me. It means nothing to people who haven't suffered."

She talked very little after this last stage of her illness began; she no longer complained or lamented, but toward Oswald her manner became strange and dark. She had certain illusions; the noise overhead she now attributed entirely to her husband. "Ah, there, he's beginning it again," she would say. "He'll wear me down in the end. Oh, let me be buried in the king's highway!"

When Oswald lifted her, or did anything for her now, she was careful to thank him in a guarded, sometimes a cringing tone. "It's bitter enough that I should have to take service from you—you whom I have loved so well," I heard her say to him.

When she asked us to use candles for light during our watches, and to have no more of the electric light she hated, she said accusingly, at him rather than to him: "At least let me die by candlelight; that is not too much to ask."

Father Fay came to see her almost daily now. His visits were long, and she looked forward to them. I was, of course, not in her room when he was there, but if he met me in the corridor he stopped to speak to me, and once he walked down the street with me talking of her. He was a young man, with a fresh face and pleasant eyes, and he was deeply interested in Myra. "She's a most unusual woman, Mrs. Henshawe," he said when he was walking down the street beside me. Then he added, smiling quite boyishly: "I wonder whether some of the saints of the early Church weren't a good deal like her. She's not at all modern in her make-up, is she?"

During those days and nights when she talked so little, one felt that Myra's mind was busy all the while—that it was even abnormally active, and occasionally one got a clue to what occupied it. One night when I was giving her her codeine she asked me a question.

"Why is it, do you suppose, Nellie, that candles are in themselves religious? Not when they are covered by shades, of course—I mean the flame of a candle. Is it because the Church began in the catacombs, perhaps?"

At another time, when she had been lying like a marble figure for a long while, she said in a gentle, reasonable voice:

"Ah, Father Fay, that isn't the reason! Religion is different from everything else; *because in religion seeking is finding.*"

She accented the word "seeking" very strongly, very deeply. She seemed to say that in other searchings it might be the object of the quest that brought satisfaction, or it might be something incidental that one got on the way; but in religion, desire was fulfillment, it was the seeking itself that rewarded.

One of those nights of watching stands out in my memory as embracing them all, as being the burden and telling the tale of them all. Myra had had a very bad day, so both Oswald and I were sitting up with her. After midnight she was quiet. The candles were burning as usual, one in her alcove. From my chair by the open window I could see her bed. She had been motionless for more than an hour, lying on her back, her eyes closed. I thought she was asleep. The city outside was as still as the room in which we sat. The sick woman began to talk to herself, scarcely above a whisper, but with perfect distinctness; a voice that was hardly more than a soft, passionate breath. I seemed to hear a soul talking.

"I could bear to suffer . . . so many have suffered. But why must it be like this? I have not deserved it. I have been true in friendship; I have faithfully nursed others in sickness. . . . Why must I die like this, alone with my mortal enemy?"

Oswald was sitting on the sofa, his face shaded by his hand. I looked at him in affright, but he did not move or shudder. I felt my hands grow cold and my forehead grow moist with dread. I had never heard a human voice utter such a terrible judgment upon all one hopes for.

As I sat on through the night, after Oswald had gone to catch a few hours of sleep, I grew calmer; I began to understand a little what she meant, to sense how it was with her. Violent natures like hers sometimes turn against themselves . . . against themselves and all their idolatries.

6

ON THE following day Mrs. Henshawe asked to be given the Sacrament. After she had taken it she seemed easier in mind and body. In the afternoon she told Henshawe to go to his office and begged me to leave her and let her sleep. The nurse we had sent away that day at her urgent request. She wanted to be cared for by one of the nursing Sisters from the convent from now on, and Father Fay was to bring one to-morrow.

I went to my room, meaning to go back to her in an hour, but once on my bed I slept without waking. It was dark when I heard Henshawe knocking on my door and calling to me. As I opened it, he said in a despairing tone: "She's gone, Nellie, she's gone!"

I thought he meant she had died. I hurried after him down the corridor and into her room. It was empty. He pointed to her empty bed. "Don't you see? She has gone, God knows where!"

"But how could she? A woman so ill? She must be somewhere in the building."

"I've been all over the house. You don't know her, Nellie. She can do anything she wills. Look at this."

On the desk lay a sheet of note paper scribbled in lead pencil: *Dear Oswald: my hour has come. Don't follow me. I wish to be alone. Nellie knows where there is money for masses.*" That was all. There was no signature.

We hurried to the police station. The chief sent a messenger out to the men on the beat to warn them to be on the watch for a distraught woman who had wandered out in delirium. Then we went to Father Fay. "The Church has been on her mind for a long while," said Henshawe. "It is one of her delusions that I separated her from the Church. I never meant to."

The young priest knew nothing. He was distressed, and offered to help us in our search, but we thought he had better stay at home on the chance that she might come to him.

When we got back to the hotel it was after eleven o'clock. Oswald said he could not stay indoors; I must be there within call, but he would go back to help the police.

After he left I began to search Mrs. Henshawe's room. She had worn her heavy coat and her furs, though the night was warm. When I found that the pair of Austrian blankets was missing, I felt I knew where she had gone. Should I try to get Oswald at the police station? I sat down to think it over. It seemed to me that she ought to be allowed to meet the inevitable end in the way she chose. A yearning strong enough to lift that ailing body and drag it out into the world again should have its way.

At five o'clock in the morning Henshawe came back with an officer and a Negro cabman. The driver had come to the station and reported that at six last night a lady, with her arms full of wraps, had signalled him at the side door of the hotel, and told him to drive her to the boat landing. When they were nearing the landing, she said she did not mean to stop there, but wanted to go farther up the shore, giving him clear directions. They reached the cliff she had indicated. He helped her out of the cab, put her rugs under the tree for her, and she gave him a ten-dollar gold piece and dismissed him. He protested that the fare was too much, and that he was afraid of getting into trouble if he left her there. But she told him a friend was going to meet her, and that it would be all right. The lady had, he said, a very kind, coaxing way with her. When he went to the stable to put up his horse, he heard that the police were looking for a woman who was out of her head, and he was frightened. He went home and talked it over with his wife, who sent him to report at headquarters.

The cabman drove us out to the headland,

and the officer insisted upon going along. We found her wrapped in her blankets, leaning against the cedar trunk, facing the sea. Her head had fallen forward; the ebony crucifix was in her hands. She must have died peacefully and painlessly. There was every reason to believe she had lived to see the dawn. While we watched beside her, waiting for the undertaker and Father Fay to come, I told Oswald what she had said to me about longing to behold the morning break over the sea, and it comforted him.

7

ALTHOUGH she had returned so ardently to the faith of her childhood, Myra Henshawe never changed the clause in her will, which requested that her body should be cremated, and her ashes buried "in some lonely and unfrequented place in the mountains, or in the sea."

After it was all over, and her ashes sealed up in a little steel box, Henshawe called me into her room one morning, where he was packing her things, and told me he was going to Alaska.

"Oh, not to seek my fortune," he said, smiling. "That is for young men. But the steamship company have a place for me in their office there. I have always wanted to go, and now there is nothing to hold me. This poor little box goes with me; I shall scatter her ashes somewhere in those vast waters. And this I want you to keep for remembrance." He dropped into my hands the necklace of carved amethysts she had worn on the night I first saw her.

"And, Nellie——" He paused before me with his arms folded, standing exactly as he stood behind Modjeska's chair in the moonlight on that New Year's night; standing like a statue, or a sentinel, I had said then, not knowing what it was I felt in his attitude; but now I knew it meant indestructible constancy . . . almost indestructible youth. "Nellie," he said, "I don't want you to remember her as she was here. Remember her as she was when you were with us on Madison Square, when she was herself, and we were happy. Yes, happier than it falls to the lot of most mortals to be. After she was stricken, her recollection of those things darkened. Life was hard for her, but it was glorious, too; she had such beautiful friendships. Of course, she was absolutely unreasonable when she was jealous. Her suspicions were sometimes—almost fantastic." He smiled and brushed his forehead with the tips of his fingers, as if the memory of her jealousy was pleasant still, and perplexing still. "But that was just Molly Driscoll! I'd rather have been clawed by her, as she used to say, than petted by any other woman I've ever known. These last years it's seemed to me that I was nursing the mother of the girl who ran away with me. Nothing ever took that girl from me. She was a wild, lovely creature, Nellie. I wish you could have seen her then."

Several years after I said good-bye to him, Oswald Henshawe died in Alaska. I have still the string of amethysts, but they are unlucky. If I take them out of their box and wear them, I feel all evening a chill over my heart. Sometimes, when I have watched the bright beginning of a love story, when I have seen a common feeling exalted into beauty by imagination, generosity, and the flaming courage of youth, I have heard again that strange complaint breathed by a dying woman into the stillness of night, like a confession of the soul: "Why must I die like this, alone with my mortal enemy!"

WILLA CATHER (1873-1947) was born near Winchester, Virginia. When she was ten, her family moved from the peace of Virginia to the wild prairies of Nebraska. She was graduated from the University of Nebraska at twenty-one, and did newspaper work and teaching in Pittsburgh, Pennsylvania, for the next few years. She published a book of verse, *April Twilights,* in 1903, and a book of short stories, *The Troll Garden,* in 1905. They were followed, over the years, by twelve novels, including *Death Comes for the Archbishop* and *Shadows on the Rock;* four volumes of short stories, and two volumes of essays. A collection, *Five Stories,* by Willa Cather, with an article by George N. Kates, is included in the *Vintage* series. Willa Cather was awarded the Pulitzer Prize for fiction in 1923.

THE TEXT of this book was set on the Linotype in FAIRFIELD, a type face designed by the distinguished American artist and engraver, Rudolph Ruzicka. This type displays the sober and sane qualities of a master craftsman whose talent has long been dedicated to clarity. Rudolph Ruzicka was born in Bohemia in 1883 and came to America in 1894. He has designed and illustrated many books and has created a considerable list of individual prints in a variety of techniques.